From the Bram Stoker Award-nominated author of
A REQUIEM FOR DEAD FLIES.

Everyone has done something evil.

Frank is planning to murder his ex-wife. Working a construction job by day and driving a cab by night, Frank is slowly falling apart just trying to make ends meet. He's poisoned by the toxic relationship with the mother of his children; all for the sake of staying in their lives. But the more he gives, the more she takes away, until he's stripped of everything. And when she finally files the restraining order to keep him away from his kids, Frank is pushed over the brink of sanity. The ex-Mrs. Blake deserves to die, and Frank buys the gun and puts his plan into motion.

Malcolm owns a bar in downtown Portland. In his decades of running MacAuley's of Scotland, he's seen every form of sin and iniquity the city has to offer. But Mal has his own sins to hide from. His past life as a World War II pilot, and the death of innocent people he inadvertently caused has always haunted him. It's been the catalyst for his downward spiral of sin and degradation. Until he realizes that he's marked for damnation. A man can only live so long and run so far from the past…

Both men are on the brink of darkness until the Angel of Death pays one of them a visit. Salvation is at hand. But how far will one man go to save himself? Can he save his friend from the very same fate?

THE ANGEL OF DEATH

PETER N. DUDAR

First Edition

ISBN: 1-938644-15-8
ISBN-13: 978-1-938644-15-3

Nightscape Press, LLP
http://www.nightscapepress.com

This book is dedicated in loving memory to

Lt. Col. Todd Clark

Who served his country with honor and died a hero.

INTRODUCTION

It's funny how life works sometimes.

I originally wrote *The Angel of Death* in 1996. It was one year after I left New York and moved to Maine. I was engaged at the time, but my wife Amy (my then-fiancé) was still living with her parents. I had a studio apartment on Oak Street, and in that tiny little box on the fourth floor I spent all my free time learning how to be a writer. I didn't have a computer back then, but I did have Amy's Sony word processor (which, thankfully had a hard-disk drive for file backup), and on it, during my first year of writing I produced one failed novel and a dozen failed short stories. Back in those days, the only places I submitted my work to were magazines that told you where to send your manuscripts via snail mail, where they would fester in slush piles for around half a year before your self-addressed envelope was returned to you with a form-letter rejection slip.

Around that time I was heavily into reading the entire Stephen King library (since I was now a Mainer, I felt obligated). That year I was reading King's novella collection *Different Seasons*. If you aren't familiar with this work, it's the tome that yielded film adaptions of *Apt Pupil, The Shawshank Redemption*, and *Stand By Me*. I fell in love with this book and still revere it to be King's best writing. But the fourth story...

The Breathing Method concerns a doomed mother-to-be who delivers her child under the most horrific of circumstances. While the odds are astronomically against such a horrid nativity, it's still a wonderfully compelling tale because the mother's story is only *half* the story. The rest of the story concerns the narrator and his involvement with a kind of gentleman's club, where the members convene basically to tell stories. In the place where the meetings are held, there is a plaque that reads, "It is the tale, not he who tells it." This sentence has stood out for me more than any other line King has ever written. For me, this line is an admission from my favorite author. It's King saying, "Hey, I just work here. I'm not the main attraction."

When I finished reading the story, I turned on the Sony and typed out that line as a quote to start my story. And then I just started writing.

I was twenty-four years old, and at the time I knew very little about life and had very little experience living. Very few people do at that age, particularly if they've been sequestered into four years of college life and then regurgitated into the real world scrambling to find a steady job with a steady income. So when it came time to develop my characters, I knew that I really wanted them to live and breathe the way they do in King's stories. Particularly with Mal, the owner of my fictitious bar who needed a back story that included time in military service. I found myself interviewing both of my grandfathers, who had each served in World War II. I took pages and pages of notes on a yellow legal pad. And for further reference, I interviewed Amy's grandfather as well. The result of my homework is a composite sketch made from all three of them. Many of the details I've listed are true accounts of their time in the service. I'm greatly indebted to them for their help, and remain delighted that they were pleased to share their life so openly and freely.

While I was writing the story, Amy's parents purchased her a new computer. She helped me set up an email account and got me into the crazy world of fast-paced internet communication (I say this tongue-in-cheek…back then it was dial-up modem, which was slower than molasses in January and tied up the phone line if anyone tried to call.) I was finally able to start visiting websites and searching for a greater variety of places to send my stories. Eventually I found an open submission call for an anthology called *The Midnighters' Club*, which was being edited by Ronald J. Horsley. When I completed the original manuscript for *The Angel of Death*, I sent him a copy via snail mail. He replied with an email saying that he liked the story very much, but there were elements still missing from it. I read his notes on the story (back then it was only a short story, weighing in at only five or six thousand words) and went back to work on it.

By the time I'd finished, the story ran way too long for inclusion, and Ron had to give a pass on it.

I was crushed. This particular piece is and remains my best piece of writing. But back then chapbooks were pretty much unheard of. So I abandoned the piece altogether and it sat on a hard disk that was only formatted for a Sony word processor. It stayed there for a dozen years.

There came a point where I realized that I had written more than sixty short stories or so. The revelation came when I was organizing some story files I had saved on old computer disks, with an eye toward putting together a collection I'd hope to sell and publish. When it hit me that I had some stories still stored on a disk that belonged solely to the word processor, I found myself scrambling to find a way to convert those files to save on our new hard drive. I found myself reading the stories I wrote that first year in my studio apartment. Many of them were flat-out terrible; poorly executed by a novice still learning the craft. But when I reached *The Angel of Death*, I was floored. The story held up over time, and it reflected the true craftsmanship of a real writer. But as Uncle Stevie says, "It is the tale, not he who tells it."

I put together a collection of my stories, and included *Angel* as an anchor story. The collection was called *Shadows in the Graveyard*, and it originally included all of my published works and a lot of works that seriously had no business ever being published. In the end it never sold because I hadn't established a name for myself and nobody was going to take a risk on an unknown author. So it stayed on my hard drive, and once again *Angel* was forgotten.

Between then and now, the small press exploded onto the scene. Publishing houses like Cemetery Dance were suddenly putting out chapbooks by their big-name authors, and the results were pretty spectacular. And with the birth of Kindle and the instant download, customers were now able to access new material from their favorite writers within seconds. What also makes this attractive is that most readers now have a very short attention span (not to be insulting...I'm right there with ya) and a very limited time for reading. Chapbooks are quite terrific; when done right they offer great cover art, a compelling story with the fat trimmed out, and are either lovingly collectable for us bibliophiles or easily parted with once the reader is done with it. As Tony the Tiger would say, "They're Grrr-reat!"

Seventeen years after it was written, *The Angel of Death* finally found a home with Nightscape Press. This is the house that published my debut novel, *A Requiem for Dead Flies* last summer, so when Bob Wilson asked me if I had anything he could have a look at, I dug out *Angel* and gave it a look over. Rereading it filled me with immense pleasure and satisfaction. I love this story, and I love the memories it evokes for me. It was me as a young man, spending hot summer nights in my lonely apartment drinking whiskey and clacking away on a word processor in a way my heroes did before me (even if *they* did their work on typewriters, which had to be an insufferable pain in the ass). It was me *finally* getting it right.

God, I miss those days.

One last thing: you will notice the whole chronological dilemma. This was written in 1996, which would have made all the sense in the world for a World War II vet to be at the age he is in the story, and conversely the age of the narrator, Frank Blake, with his own children finally reaching the age of 18. So for you, the reader, keep in mind that everything in the story should be retroactively dated so that your brain won't explode trying to figure out the past-present time continuum. Mmm-kay? Wunderbar!

As always, I'd like to thank my fan base: Barbara Lovenberg, Linda Martin, Elizabeth Burke, Debbie LaFrance, Nicky Merrill, April Hawks, Jennifer Libby, Jim Costello, Jody Smith, Darby May, and all those other folks who supported me from the beginning. Also, a large shout of thanks to fellow authors L.L. Soares, Nick Cato, Scott Goudsward, Bracken MacLeod, Peter Giglio, Joe McKinney, Tracy Carbone, Dan Keohane, Michael Collings, Tony Tremblay, my NeCon family, and of course, Stephen King.

And, as always, to my lovely wife Amy: Thank you for being the light in my world of darkness.

It is the tale, not he who tells it.

-Stephen King

1

The name on my hack license reads Francis Blake, but most folks call me Frank. I've always hated the name...sounds so goddamn prissy, ya know? Not the name you'd want as a cab driver. It almost demands your fare to take notice, to ask about it, and in some cases to assume you are as physically weak as your name is. Those are the people that try to stiff you. The last person to try that with me was in for a rude awakening, but I'll tell you about that later.

I've been driving a cab in the Greater Portland Area for five years now, and coincidentally, if one were to examine the timeline of my life, that is one year less than I've been divorced. It isn't my primary source of income, God no. My day job is with the Harding Construction Company. Aside from my hack license, I'm certified to operate bulldozers, forklifts, and other heavy machinery. I make pretty good money there, but my ex-wife takes most of it in alimony and child support.

It was an ugly divorce, I must admit. She'd been having an affair. She was sleeping with a younger man (she wouldn't tell me whom, said it wasn't important) for some time, and finally he'd talked her into leaving me. I was devastated, thoroughly heart wrenched. She had made a cuckold of me. Cuckold; now there's a word of notoriety if ever there was one. It's used in all walks of literature, from Shakespeare to Dickens. Hearing it and being it are two different things. It intertwines two separate feelings. The first is the pain of loss and the empty hole it tears in your heart. The second is the humiliation of being played for a fool. For over a year she was telling me how she loved me while she was fucking some other guy behind my back. I suppose I believed that marriage was supposed to last forever and the words, "I love you," were something you said only when you meant it. I hired a private investigator to find out who the man was. Turns out she was leaving me for a lawyer. And wouldn't you know, he represented her in our divorce case (in spite of the whole "conflict of interest" business).

I demanded custody of our two children. I didn't care about anything else. The house, our savings, they meant nothing to me. My lawyer informed me that my chances were better than fair of obtaining custody due to her infidelity. Neither of us was prepared when she sat up on the witness stand and without a hint of shame declared that I had beaten her and my children, and that I had a problem with alcohol. By the time she'd finished, my good name was ruined, although none of it was true. So, not only had she made a cuckold of me, she took my two children. On top of that, she was awarded my house, sixty percent of our savings and possessions, my car, alimony and child support. I wanted to kill her.

And to show you how slick her lawyer/boyfriend was, he escorted her hand in hand from the courtroom, and moved into my home immediately. And I ended up paying the legal costs for both sides.

My lawyer told me that the court favors the mother in most cases, and even if she hadn't lied, there would have been the possibility of her keeping the children, although she was the one to ruin the marriage. I did get custody of the children for one weekend a month, and for that I was thankful.

As I've said, that was six years ago.

I couldn't afford to survive on the money I was earning at Harding. My paychecks were minimal after Uncle Sam took his cut and my ex-wife took hers. I went to the DMV and applied for my hack license and afterwards applied for a job at Fat Eddie's Cabs. Fat Eddie was short on drivers, and hired me on the spot.

Fat Eddie lives up to his name. He's a big, big man with a balding head usually covered with perspiration. He usually wears baggy black sweatpants and some sports team T-shirt, and leather high-top sneakers like the basketball players wear. He's bulky and greasy looking—the kind of man even the prostitutes turn down. Despite his outward appearance he is a pleasant, genial man. When I applied for the job, I explained my situation to him, and he was sympathetic. On top of this, he has a tremendous sense of humor, although his puns are dreadful.

He started me on the 10 p.m. till 2 a.m. shift. This is what he refers to as the "drunk" shift. College kids and the local riffraff usually leave bars around this time, too drunk to drive. I worked this shift for roughly seven months, on top of my day job. The tips sucked and the fares were nothing more than young punks too inebriated to pronounce their own names. I spent countless nights cleaning vomit (and on occasion other bodily excretions) out of the back of my cab. All the while I thought of my ex and her lawyer lover fucking in my old bed. Doing it out of wedlock, no less, with my children in the house. If he were to marry her, I'd be off the hook with alimony. I'd only have to pay child support. I guess I knew deep down that he wouldn't marry her. He'd only use her up until something younger came along.

My nights doing the "drunk" shift came to an end with my first and last fare stiff.

What had happened was this. I'd had a bad day. I spent the whole of it stewing over my situation and how utterly helpless I felt. My ex was supposed to let me take the kids for the weekend. *My* weekend. She was supposed to have them dressed, their overnight bags packed, and waiting on the doorstep by noon. I had taken the weekend off from both jobs to be with them. I'd made plans to take them to the movies, dinner, the works. Quality time with my children. *My* children! I was waiting outside my old house by quarter of, sitting in a cab that Fat Eddie let me take for the weekend since *she* now owned my car. By quarter after, I got out of the cab, walked up the steps and rang the doorbell, and confirmed my suspicions. Nobody was home.

I waited three hours, the rage growing inside like a volcano of red heat. The old fantasies of killing her came flooding back. All the different ways to do it. How I could make it look like an accident. And then I had an epiphany. An enlightenment. I realized that a plan was already being formed in my subconscious that somehow the rest of my brain hadn't quite clued in on. I was absolutely going to kill her. I turned the key in the ignition of the old cab and sped home.

Naturally, there was a message waiting on my answering machine. The snobby voice of my ex-wife came on, pronouncing how sorry she was and that she'd have to reschedule my weekend with the kids; not really giving me a reason, just an "I can get away with this and there's nothing you can do about it," tone of voice. What I did to deserve such contempt I'll never know.

So I went to work that night, driving my cab in the Old Port, as always. Picking up miscellaneous college students, vagrants, et cetera and dreaming about killing my ex. It would have to be after my youngest child turned 18...don't want the kids ending up with foster parents, or worse yet, raised by my ex's parents. They had no love for me, I can tell you that... They'd always wanted their daughter to marry a doctor or a lawyer. I didn't fit the mold they were looking for in a son-in-law. And I certainly didn't want them taking their hatred out on my children after I'd offed their precious daughter.

I'd planned on driving until 2 a.m., but I picked up my last fare at 1: 15. A drunken college kid walking down Congress Street flagged me down, and asked me to drive him to the campus out in Gorham. A healthy fare that would have been, had he not tried to stiff me. I was already pissed off, and I figured a trip to Gorham would put me in a better mood. My fare fell asleep in the back of the cab (although looking back, I'm not sure he really was sleeping) and remained silent until we hit Gorham.

He bailed out right when I pulled up to the stop light by the supermarket.

I had been daydreaming about killing her (this time, I imagined handcuffing her to the bed and stuffing a hand grenade inside that big mouth of hers) and was shaken to reality when I heard the back door slam shut behind me.

I was out in a flash. I never even bothered to shut the motor off. It ran idly at the stop light through the whole ordeal. I caught him in the supermarket parking lot. My hand had reached out and caught a lock of his sweaty blond hair. His neck jerked back as his legs continued forward, and he toppled backwards on his ass.

And I beat him.

With all the bottled up hatred and rage that was reserved for my ex-wife, I beat him within inches of his own death. I smashed his skull into the rough asphalt of the parking lot as he blubbered and wailed how sorry he was. He screamed for help all the while I was battering him, my arms flailing in solid blows against his face, his chest, his stomach. I showed him absolutely no trace of mercy as the cuts and bruises doubled, then tripled. I lost track of the time frame all this happened in. Someone must have called the police. I the heard the wail of sirens and saw the flashing lights as the cruiser entered the parking lot, but that didn't stop me. I had, by this time, mangled the boy's face, breaking his nose, blackening his eyes, knocking some of his teeth out of his otherwise perfect smile. It took two officers to pull me off.

The officers never so much as handcuffed me. The reason why was this...I was crying. Not blubbering like the college kid was. Just tears streaming down my face. One of the officers asked me if the kid had stiffed his fare. The knot in my throat left me speechless, and I could only nod my head.

The other officer went over to the boy and lifted him to his feet. I didn't hear the whole conversation, but I picked up bits and pieces. The officer told him that if he pressed charges, I could press countercharges and have him arrested for theft of service and public drunkenness, both of which carried jail time, a fine, and a permanent spot on his record. The boy declined, naturally. He'd paid enough already. Looking back, I'm not sure if the officer told him this to save himself paperwork, or make an example of the boy to the other students. Or maybe it was because I was a grown man bawling my eyes out like a baby over the whole situation. I must have looked so pathetic. They let me off with a warning, and the officer who spoke with the boy proposed that I seek professional counseling.

I took the rest of that weekend off, and when I reported for duty at Fat Eddie's on Monday night, Eddie pulled me into his office and asked me to explain.

When I finished, he switched me from the "drunk" shift to the "tie" shift.

Simply stated, the "tie" shift runs from 8 p.m. till midnight. The fares are mostly business men from the downtown area; suits and ties representing the government, legal establishments, bankers, store managers, et cetera... Some getting out of work late, some stopping in at the local watering holes (not like the dance clubs or sports bars the college students usually hang out in). They are well mannered, rarely noisy, and tip generously. And in some instances, you can pick up good investment secrets and even a hot tip on a horse race at Scarborough Downs. I thanked Fat Eddie and the sweet Lord above for getting me away from the "drunk" shift.

And guess who my first fare of the night was...

My ex-wife's lawyer.

I picked him up outside Town Hall. He opened the door and shoved his brief case in, and barked out my old address. Can you believe that? The killing fantasies rushed through my head like a tidal wave. He was loosening his tie when he glanced up at the rearview mirror and saw my eyes staring at him. But by that time, I had pushed the "automatic door lock" switch and was on my way.

He tried not to act surprised, but the man had no poker face. I could read right through him that he was extremely nervous to be in the same cab with the man he'd so perfectly fucked over; in taking my wife, my home, my family, my money. His eyes were fixed on mine in the rearview mirror. He cleared his throat and tried to speak.

"S... SS... So, you're driving a cab now?" He choked. What a little pussy. Looking back, I think I would have loved to catch him in the act of fucking my wife. The little puke would probably have shit himself. And I probably would have killed the both of them, and the whole messy thing would have been over. As it were, I played it real cool.

"Yeah...I have to pay the bills somehow." I was smiling at him, and I could see him shift around uncomfortably.

"That... that's great. I'm glad you're taking charge of your life."

"That ain't all I'm gonna take charge of, friend."

He'd turned to jelly. I could hear his stomach growling underneath that cheap-ass suit. I was elated. The whole college-kid-fare-stiffing ordeal was entirely forgotten. I wanted this man to squirm.

"Are you threatening me?" he asked, his voice on the verge of tears. He was trying to sound as though he could really fuck me over if I were. But then I suppose I really didn't care at the time.

"If I wanted to hurt you, I would have done it by now. But I imagine you're still worried, seeing how you stole my whole life away from me..."

"I did no such thing!" He was terrified and trying to scoff at my last comment as a means of making himself feel more in charge of the situation.

"Shut up, you little worm..." I hissed at him. I hadn't noticed, but my foot was slowly pushing down on the accelerator. "Because you *did*. You're sleeping with *my* wife, in *my* house, and caring for *my* children. And I'm the one who's paying for it. I suppose you think you're better than I am, with your fake Italian suit and your briefcase. I bet it feels so powerful to screw over decent people so easily!"

He was hanging his head, no longer making eye contact with me. I could tell by his reflection in the mirror he was trembling.

"...But the worst part is that you let that bitch lie on the stand. I never laid a finger on her or my children. And I am NOT an alcoholic!"

"Let me out," he whispered hoarsely. "Pull over and let me out."

"I don't think so, friend! Tell me...where were my kids this weekend when they were supposed to be with me?" The rage inside me was burning with the intensity of ten suns.

"I ... I ... ah..." He was gasping. I owned this man at this particular moment in existence. I felt like a god, like I had usurped all the power this man had used against me in the courtroom, and my cab was now my own place of judgment. And justice was no longer blind, but able to see the light.

"They weren't there, were they?" I was screaming. The windows of my cab were steaming over from my hot breath. I caught a glimpse of the speedometer. I was doing 75 down Route 302.

"Please..." he sobbed, "you're going to kill us both if you don't slow down."

"What makes you think I want to go on living?" I asked, my mouth drawn in the most sinister smile I could manage. But just the same, I slowed down a bit, in case any cops might be waiting in one of their speed traps.

His face had gone pale, as if he'd seen a ghost, and I wondered if he was weak enough to have a heart attack. Wouldn't that have been a trip? To have my wife's lover die of (almost) natural causes right in the back of my cab. I wanted it so bad, I could taste it.

He was alive, though, by the time I'd reached my old house in Windham. It had been the second time I'd seen it in the course of a week. I remembered how much hatred I'd held while parked outside just a few short days ago, waiting for my kids who weren't even there. I pushed the "automatic door lock" into unlock, and watched through my rearview mirror as he threw a twenty dollar bill at me and bailed out, running up the steps and barreling through the front door. He left his briefcase in the back seat of my cab, which I was more than happy to throw off a bridge and into one of the many nameless streams that ultimately make their way into Sebago Lake.

My ex-wife phoned me between jobs the next day. She invited me to an early dinner to talk. We met at a local Denny's off Brighton Avenue and Riverside Street. She looked radiantly beautiful (at least in outward appearance) and shook my hand cordially as we sat down at the table I'd been waiting at.

"I'm sorry about you missing your weekend with the kids," she started with. "Maybe next weekend, if it's okay by you?"

"I used up all my free time last weekend," I growled back. "It'll be a whole month before I can get off from both jobs again."

"Oh, yes...Joshua mentioned you were driving a cab now. He's arranging for a new child support hearing this afternoon. With you at a higher income, your kids are eligible for more child support." Christ, the bitch wanted more money. She was more of a man than her pansy lawyer boyfriend. Here she was, already taking charge of the situation, something I would not let her do.

"If you do that, you'll regret it." I responded. I was flustered. The purpose of me working a second job was so that I could afford to live on my own. Now she was determined to take that away from me as well. I looked down at my fork and wondered how good it would feel to jam it right through her eye and into her brain. I never wanted anything more desperately in my life than to do just that.

"Oh, really? Why?" She smiled her wicked little slut smile at me. I hated her.

"Because if you do that, I'll quit both jobs and you and your faggot little lawyer friend won't get another cent."

"How noble." She was trying to call my bluff, although deep down, I wasn't bluffing. "You're willing to starve yourself to death to spite me?" She was chuckling in amusement.

"I won't starve myself to death, dear," I retorted, "I'll shoot myself to death. And if I do that, I swear to God and Christ above that I'll take you with me. There's nothing left for me to live for." There was no amusement in my voice. I came across as dead serious, and she knew it.

Two things happened after that lunch. First, she and her lawyer friend decided not to pursue hitting me up for more child support. Second, she had a restraining order placed on me to keep me away from her, her boyfriend, and my children. I lost whatever custody I had left as their father. And I was most definitely planning on killing her.

All of this is important, but it's not what I really wanted to tell you about.

My best friend died last night.

2

Malcolm MacAuley owned a bar over on Exchange Street called "MacAuley's of Scotland." During my years on the "tie" shift, I'd often pick up fares at this pub, and quite frequently, when my shift ended, I'd come in for a few drinks myself. Mal was somewhere in his seventies when he passed away last night. His death wasn't a surprise. He'd had heart and lung problems from breathing all the second hand smoke in his bar. Mal, himself, only smoked on rare occasions.

"MacAuley's of Scotland" (or "Mac's," if you're a regular as I am) is, in my own opinion, the finest bar in the city, or all of New England for that manner. It has the demeanor of the typical European pub, which gives it an edge of distinction from the other bars and watering holes around here. The building itself is actually a two-story. The top half is Mal's apartment, where he had lived since returning from World War II (double-yew, double-yew, aye-aye, as Mal would call it). The bottom floor is the bar. There is a giant picture window in the front, with a stained-glass image embedded within, depicting Mal's family crest;

a shield made up of silver-tinted glass with a lion's head carved in the center. The lion is wearing a crown of gold and a medallion around its neck in the shape of a cross. The beast is flanked by two swords criss-crossing into an X behind him, and a ribbon of scroll beneath which simply reads "MacAuley." The stained glass is done in striking color and detail, and I've often wondered how it has remained virtually unscathed by the local j.d.'s who are often quick to vandalize anything of significant beauty around here.

As you enter Mac's, the bar is to the immediate left and runs that entire side of the wall. Above the bar is an actual shield and swords that comprise Mal's family crest (no doubt the stained glass artist's model for the picture window) with the addition of an authentic plaid kilt unraveled behind it. The material is an ugly colored plaid, composed of a hideous yellow tint intertwined with red, green, and brown stripes. Mal would often brag of his lineage with the MacAuley clan, and that the kilt could still fit him, despite the horrendous beer gut he'd developed since owning the establishment.

Across the bar are scattered tables, alternating round and square so that from an overhead view, the floor looks like a checkerboard. The tables and the bar itself are made of a rich colored mahogany, but the tables all have the lion's head (complete with crown and medallion) painted on them. The surrounding walls are decorated with paintings and pictures of Scotland, and on the far wall opposite the door is Scotland's flag, prominently displayed above the men's and ladies' rooms.

To the immediate right of the door is a dart board, with a line chalked on the floor to indicate proper throwing distance. Beyond that is a pool table (although Mac's clients never use the word "pool," they refer to the game as billiards or snooker). And beyond that, filling the back right corner of the bar, is one solitary booth, with benches upholstered in a rich, red leather on either side. The table at this booth is the only one without the lion's head painted on. Instead, there is a chessboard painted on one side (Mal kept the chess pieces behind the bar; the pieces are carved out of silver for one side, and bronze for the other. The craftsmanship in sculpting these pieces is nothing short of brilliant, and would probably amass a fortune if he decided to sell them. As it were, you needed to let Mal hold your driver's license if you wanted to use them, and he'd count the pieces before giving it back to you when you were finished), and a cribbage board on the other side, with the peg holes drilled neatly into the table. The pegs were kept in a small plastic dish on the inside of the table, along with the napkin holder and coasters. You had to bring your own cards though, or you could buy a deck from Mal, who had playing cards customized with his family crest pictured on the cards, surrounded in a field of black with an additional ribbon scrolled along the top, reading, "MacAuley's of Scotland," in gold letters on red border.

And that was it. No distracting large screen televisions with sports events or local news on, no jukebox cranked up so loud you can't hear yourself speak, no glitter balls dangling from the ceiling or flashy neon lights glowing through the haze of cigarette smoke. And damned if it wasn't the most pleasant, relaxing atmosphere to be in.

It was also the clientele that made the bar what it was. Stuffy business men in expensive suits, who during normal business hours were the arrogant, no nonsense, stick-up-the-ass CEOs, bankers, lawyers (and judges in many instances), investors, etc... But when they enter Mac's, it's as if there is an invisible sign at the door reading "Please remove stick from ass before entering." The excruciating stress of business life melts away, and these people become human again. They down a few drinks and have fun, if only for a few short hours a night.

Aside from these folks, occasionally the bar has a few yuppies running amok (and they always enter in groups, as if there is safety in numbers. The yuppies are never regulars until they learn to come in alone). And even more occasionally come in the dames; the ladies either widowed and looking for company, married unhappily and looking, or single and looking for a sugar daddy to pamper them and buy them more than drinks. So the bar is like one big gentleman's club, if you will. And gentlemen they are, with their imported cigars and tumblers of brandy and gin, their free arm around the waists of women that aren't their wives. You'd think I'd stick out like a sore thumb.

But I don't. They know me by name and offer to buy me drinks when they see me walk in. When I'm on duty, I politely refuse, and take home (or to pay-by-the-hour motels in some cases), those clients that are ready to leave. And as I've said, they tip generously (to keep my mouth shut, I suspect). If I'm off duty, I'll take 'em up on their offer and tell them the latest jokes I've heard (you pick up tons driving a cab). Afterwards, I'll sit at the bar and talk with Mal.

Like most good bartenders, Mal listens with a sympathetic ear. He never offers advice (a characteristic which makes him golden in my book), and never casts judgment on you for your problems.

Thursdays and Fridays are always the busiest nights at Mac's. On these nights,

Mal has a second bartender, a fellow named Steven, and a waitress named Ursula, a stunning blonde of German dissent, helping him. Ursula is often referred to by the clientele as "bar wench," a moniker which she giggles off, even as they pat her on the ass when she turns to go fill their orders. She often wears a black miniskirt and a white blouse with ruffles around the collar, which stop just above her enormous bosom. Many of the clientele make jokes or nasty comments about what her sexual performance must be like, and often these are mentioned within earshot, but she either pretends not to notice, or when the comment is off-color enough will respond with an even more off-color retort. The rest of the crowd will laugh and often applaud when this happens, and she'll smile and walk away. Her beauty is only surpassed by her dignity.

On one occasion while I was there, a very drunk (and very rich) old man slapped a hundred dollar bill on the table and told her it was hers if she'd show him her tits. Without batting an eyelash, in front of the whole bar, she hefted her blouse and bra up and flashed her breasts at him, her nipples hard from exposure to the stale air. It happened so fast that the man who made the offer let out a weak groan and dropped his beer in his lap. The room thundered with applause as she tucked her shirt back in and picked up the hundred off the table. That night, she made at least two grand in tips.

I've never really talked with Ursula, other than a courteous salutation or a drink order if I'm away from the bar. I feel she's too attractive for a guy like me to speak to, and although she doesn't wear a wedding band or speak of a significant other, I'm sure she's making some other man very happy. At the same time, I also wonder if she's ever slept with any of the rich men that come through the door; or if she's ever had her heart broken as I have; that we might have a common bond between us. I suppose I'll always wonder.

Steve, the other bartender, has a silent air about him. He is more than knowledgeable in the art of bartending, can make any and every mixed drink known to man down to precise measurement and taste. He also knows more about vintage wines and whiskeys than any bartender in New England. When he speaks, his voice comes out in a dull monotone, and his words ring of propriety, enunciated with flawless syllables and accented voice. In all, he reminds me of a butler, and one who's gravely out of place to be in such an uncultured city. I've tried to speak with him, but unlike Mal, he does not listen well, and acts as if his only function in life is to pour drinks and collect tips. I often wonder how he gets along with Mal and Ursula; to my knowledge I cannot recall him ever speaking with them. Perhaps Steve is nothing more than a ghost, a figment of my imagination, although I've watched him pour drinks for many of the bar's patrons. It haunts me to think about it.

But Mal listens, and roughly a month ago, he listened to me tell the same story I told you about my ex-wife and her lawyer lover. And for the first time in the five years I've been friends with him, he told me a story in return. And now that he's dead, his story is more hauntingly real. It has touched a chord deep in my soul that I'm quite positive I didn't want touched; the part of my soul that questions my own mortality and the possibilities of Heaven and Hell and God and the afterlife. And it made me think twice about the plan I had been forming in that area of my brain that aches for revenge against my ex-wife.

3

As I've told you, the busiest nights are Thursdays and Fridays. The slowest night of the week is Saturday, the night every other bar in downtown Portland is jumping with kids and booze and life as the rest of the world knows it. T.G.I.F.? Hallelujah for Saturday! Saturday doesn't exist in the business day calendar, and all the CEOs, bankers, lawyers (and judges in many cases), and investors are at home with their families. For me, the "tie" shift doesn't exist on Saturdays either, and the bulk of my fares come from the Portland Jetport. I stop by Mac's when my shift ends and down a few beers before heading back to my tiny apartment over on Oak Street.

It was on a Saturday last month that all of this happened, and Mal relayed his story to me. We had been sitting in the back booth table playing cribbage. He'd been a solid fifteen pegs ahead of me, and was dealing when my ex-wife's lawyer-lover entered the bar with his arm around a younger woman that wasn't my ex-wife. I was thrilled from head to toe. Either he'd finally dumped the bitch that was my ex-wife, or was cheating on her and it was an inevitability. And in that instant when I saw him, I hoped for nothing else but for her to be at home, crying her eyes out with a broken heart. I wanted her to drown in loneliness, to hear the cold sound of solitude echo in her ears until the night seemed to draw into an abysmal eternity.

They had been dressed for a night on the town. Him in a black tuxedo with matching solid-colored tie and cummerbund, she in a slinky red evening gown barely containing her bosom as she walked. Her lipstick accentuated her evening gown perfectly, making her long hair look that much more blonde. She was a knockout.

He hadn't noticed I was there yet.

But I saw him.

"Hey, Josh! Can I give you a lift home?" I called out.

I was standing at the table now, and his eyes had finally met mine. The reaction was instantaneous. The skin of his face darkened from its normal pale hue to a burning red. His eyes dropped to the floor, and before his lovely date could make a sound, he'd grabbed her arm and whipped back out the door and into the street.

I laughed. For the first time in six years, I laughed. I laughed till my face turned as beet-red as Josh's had been moments earlier, with fat, rolling tears streaming down my face. I laughed till the air left my lungs, and my stomach began to cramp. I must have looked a sight of total lunacy, for Mal stood up and taken me by the arm, and sat me back down in my seat.

"What's so damn funny?" he asked as I brushed the tears from my eyes and took a swig of beer.

"That's the guy who's been fucking my wife," I said between giggles. "Only that ain't my wife he's with tonight."

Mal sat back in his chair and rubbed his chin contemplatively before picking up the cards he'd just dealt. I picked up my own and glanced at them, but I was too excited to actually decide yet which cards to throw in his crib.

"So she got what was coming to her..." he said finally, his eyes still on his cards as his fat fingers pulled two of them from his hand and dropped them on the table.

"No!" I said. "Not by a long shot."

"No? She must have really screwed you over, huh? What happened?"

I told him the story from start to finish, just as I've told you.

When I finished, he dropped the rest of his hand on the table. He sat back against his bench and reached into his shirt pocket for his pack of cigarettes. He thumbed one out and placed it between his lips, pulled a book of matches from his pants pocket, and lit it.

After exhaling his first puff, his eyes looked right into mine, and I saw a haunted look about them that I hadn't noticed, not in the years that I've known him.

"You want to kill her, don'tcha?"

The words hit me like a stinging slap in the face.

His eyes were still locked with mine, and I got the creepy feeling that he was looking into my soul, already knowing the answer before I could let it escape from my lips. I stuttered out my reply.

"Well, yeah...I've thought about it...not that I'd really do it..."

"But not just kill her, but to make her suffer, to be sure that she hurts just a little more than she hurt you."

My eyes dropped from his, and my cheeks still burning from laughter now singed with shame.

"...And even that's not good enough, is it? I bet you can't wait to call her and tell her what you saw in here tonight. Am I right?"

He was reading my mind like an open book, and I was beginning to shift with discomfort. I could feel the butterflies in my stomach, and droplets of sweat bead up beneath my armpits, trickling down my ribs underneath my shirt.

"She hurt me!" I uttered in a low voice, almost a whisper. Not just because she fell out of love with me, but because she had treated my life as if it were a game, and I was nothing more than a pawn, or a peg like on the cribbage board in front of me. Only she had broken the rules; she'd played dirty and rubbed my nose in it at every available opportunity. *That* was why I wanted to kill her.

Only now it didn't seem so glamorous or rewarding as I'd first imagined. Now it just seemed like I wanted to play dirty as well. And Mal read it in my face, saw it in my eyes, and knew what lurked in the dark places of my heart. In that moment I believe I hated him for it.

He flicked the growing ashes of his cigarette onto the floor before speaking again.

"Do yourself a favor, kid..." He moved his face closer, as if he was divulging some big secret he wanted no one else to hear, not that anyone was paying attention.

"Let it go."

My head shot up so that my eyes caught his again, and for a brief moment, I thought my ears deceived me.

"What?"

"Let it go." He pulled his head back, resumed his normal sitting position, and continued.

"Kid, do as the Bible says and turn the other cheek. Don't damn yourself because of her wickedness. Forgive her and let it go."

The shock of his words turned my shame into rage again. He wasn't the one going through the pain I was going through. Who the fuck was he to give me advice? Nothing more than a lousy bartender who was overstepping the boundaries of his job. I found myself raising my voice at him.

"What kind of bullshit is that?" I hissed indignantly. "Let it go...What the fuck? I can't even see my own goddamn children because of that bitch and you tell me to 'Let it go?'"

"That's your pride talking, Frank. Only you won't talk like that to the Lord when he's getting ready to make judgment." He took another drag off his cigarette and exhaled, blowing the smoke across the table and into my face. It burned my eyes.

"If there is a Lord!" I retorted.

"Oh, there's a Lord," he said. "I won't get to meet him, but you," he pointed at me with the lit end of his cigarette and his index finger. "...you still have a chance."

His eyes filled with that haunted look again, and it scared me. Scared me to the pit of my stomach, so that my flesh crawled with goose pimples and the skin of my scrotum shriveled up. I now felt haunted as well.

"I want to tell you a story," he began...

4

"I was a pilot during double-yew, double-yew, aye-aye. I flew the B-24s, you know, the big planes they used to bomb the bejeesus out of the Germans? Well, I was stationed in Calacundi, India for thirteen months. And during that time I must have flown well over one hundred missions. Not the A-bomb, that was delivered by a B-17 called the 'Enola Gay'...No, we'd drop smaller bombs. Hit military targets and so forth. We gave Hitler and his boys more shit than they'd ever dreamed we could.

"When you entered Calacundi, you didn't come by air, but by ship. So you'd catch a ride with the gunships up the Hooghly River into Calacundi. Me, I came on a ship called the USS Greely...a hospital ship rather than a gunboat. We left port in Australia and traveled up the Indian Ocean, and that was some of the roughest goddamned travel you could ever make. There was an Air Force base there in Calacundi, just outside Calcutta itself, where I stayed for my thirteen months. It was set at the edge of the desert, on a strip of flat land that was originally nothing more than tarred down runways, which ended up getting paved over just after I got there. It was a horrible location for a base, with sand getting in the jets and blasting you like sandpaper when the wind picked up. But it was fairly neutral territory and fairly centered between the fronts in Europe and Japan. So they threw together a couple of makeshift hangers for whatever repairs and service the jets needed, and the bulk of the jets sat beneath huge canvas tarps when they weren't being used—although most were in use on a daily basis, unless we were short on pilots or conducting drills or whatnot.

"My daily routine consisted of calisthenics—which was usually minimal due to the scorching heat—breakfast, mission briefing, and then it was up, up and away. The grounds crew took care of loading us with fuel and ammunition and so forth, so all we had to do was go drop bombs on our specified locations. The term they used for these missions was "Pin-point Bombing". Those were the missions I was assigned.

"I was a good pilot. I was better than good. I was the best. The boys in the Luftwaffe knew my name, and in turn called me "The Scottish Lion." I had gained a notoriety that equaled the "Red Baron's," in the first World War. That notoriety held a price for me that I never expected to pay. It sealed my fate.

"Aside from the burning heat and sand of the desert, and the poverty of the country and its people we were using, I was happy. I was good at something, although that something was murder disguised as war. I killed people, plain and simple. And looking back, I suppose the thought of going home was something I didn't pay much attention to.

"The enemy knew my name. I saw my own name in all kinds of European newspapers, and I was pretty damn full of myself for it. I'd strut around camp and boast about my successful missions to the other pilots, most of which would run a handful of missions and be shipped off to some other part of the war. And of course, some were shot down and went home in body bags. Yessir, I was hot shit, and Danger was my middle name.

"The majority of my missions were flown over Europe, particularly Germany and

Austria. And in some instances I could see the death camps, you know, the concentration camps that made Hitler and his yahoos so famous, or infamous if you will. I'd often do flybys, if the airspace was open and secured from enemy fighters. The B-24s were no match to the Messerschmitts in a dogfight, let me tell you. The B-24s—or 'The Liberators' as they were called—were too big and bulky for tactical maneuvering compared to the German gunships. So I'd drop altitude and buzz by, and my ship would be traveling so fast that I'd see only a fraction of a glance of the walls surrounding the compound, a red blur of the Nazi flags depicting the dreaded swastika, and a handful of military vehicles that could have passed for ants at my point of view. But I saw 'em. And I never thought twice of the horrors going on there because I knew that if I let it bother me, I could put an end to them by dropping my bombs on them. Besides, I was busy enough with my missions, and didn't have time for it anyway.

"So there I was in my thirteenth month, the success rate of my missions untouchable, my place in history filed neatly under the moniker "the Scottish

Lion." Scottish Lion...can you believe that shit? As if the world needed a hero like me. I'd spent my first four months in the service praying to God for safety before my missions, and praying for forgiveness afterwards. And in those first four months, my success rate was just over fifty percent. The crew that flew with me in my jet changed every other day, and most of them weren't very bright. They followed orders poorly, and as a result, the bombs either dropped too early or too late. To compensate for this, I'd dip my plane below the appropriate altitude for bombing. And my success rate started climbing.

"This was, of course, against regulation. So, I'd have to doctor my radio transmissions and my log book before turning it in at the end of my missions. My superior officers knew, of course. But they were so damn pleased with my success rate they often overlooked my "strategies." Hell, they'd even joke about it over drinks in the Officers' Club. And I'd raise my glass and drink along with 'em.

"So when the first four months became the next four months, my prayers shifted from praying for safety to praying for successful missions. The forgiveness prayer ceased all together. It was War, after all, and I was doing my job just like the German Storm Troopers were doing theirs. My success rate continued to climb, and I was promoted to Major. Major Malcolm, the 'Scottish Lion.' Christ, whoever thought up that nickname should be shot. At the time I loved it, and hand painted a lion on the back fin of my jet. It was wearing a kilt of the MacAuley plaid and blowing a bagpipe. Someone snapped a picture of me painting it and sent it into *Life* Magazine. They published it in a segment about the American Armed

Forces, and all of America got to see the 'Scottish Lion' for themselves. I had the picture framed, and hung it over there behind the bar. I'm sure I've seen you look at it at least a dozen times.

"It was in the third four months when the close calls began. You see, by that time I believed I was invincible. The prayers stopped outright—I no longer needed a god to watch over me. There is a word for what darkness was growing inside of me. Hubris. More than just the defiance of God, but the belief that I was Godlike myself. I was one cocky sonofawhore, let me tell you. I'd dive way the hell below the regulation bombing altitudes, down so close to the earth that ground fire could have easily left me for dead over the front line. I would dive so close that my crew often joked nervously about famed Colonel Prescott's line, 'Hold your fire till you see the whites of their eyes!' And it was only a matter of time before my plane would be hit.

"On September 24th, 1944—in the start of my thirteenth month—I received my mission to bomb several military targets in Berlin herself. It was the icing on the cake, let me tell you. My head was in the clouds before my jet left the runway. But before my plane went into the air, I went into the rear of the plane and addressed my crew. We knelt down together, and I said a prayer. I broke through my hubris. I don't know if it was out of sincerity or superstition or whatever, but there I was praying beside my men. The prayer I said sounded like this...

"'Heavenly Father, Please keep us safe in our most holy mission. May our bombs cease the tyranny of the enemy, and may they bring peace to the land which we fight so valiantly for. Amen.'

"And then it was up, up and away.

"We never made it to Berlin. There had been an air strike waiting for us just over the German border, and we were chased across the European sky like a rabbit being hunted by a pack of dogs. We'd radioed headquarters and requested a counterattack team, and as if someone in Heaven above were watching us, a squadron of American gunships intercepted out of the northern sky.

"But by then, we'd been hit. Our wing had taken a spitfire of enemy ammunition, and we were losing altitude fast. And worse, it looked like we'd land behind the front line, and be stranded in enemy territory.

"So I gave the order.

"'Dump everything out of the ship; anything that's weighing us down, get rid of it!'

"My men dumped every last bomb. Dropped them furiously out the ammo bay in the bottom of the plane. I can still hear them bitches whistling their way down to the earth, and see them lighting up the ground like the morning sun. And you could hear them detonate, which was entirely impossible over the roar of the engines and hissing wind of the stratosphere bristling around us. But our plane was significantly lighter, and we'd soared out of enemy territory to safety at a distantly closer American base than the one I called headquarters.

"Now, when you are the leader of any group of men, their morale is in proportion to your own. They depend on you to be strong and fearless, even when you're so afraid you've all but pissed your pants. I was considerably shaken up. Christ, it was too close for comfort, and we were goddamn lucky to be alive and breathing. So I addressed my men and congratulated them on a job well done in getting us out alive. I then exited my plane and went to the infirmary, where I collapsed into mild shock.

"When I awoke, a general was standing by my side. He was an older fellow, with a bald head adorned around the base with a faint patch of gray hairs, which matched his mustache and eyebrows. I threw my arm up in a salute which he waved off as he sat down on the edge of my bed.

"'Son,' he said in a sad but pleasant voice, 'this isn't an official briefing. Far from it. I have your record on my desk, and I've seen from it that you're a hell of a pilot. I heard your radio transmissions, and I know you were in a hell of a jam up there today. It's a miracle you and your boys made it back.'

"'Yessir,' I said. My throat was dry, and my voice came out rough and crackled.

I knew something was wrong. I had to have really fucked up to have this general speaking to me.

"'And you didn't have much of a choice unloading your cargo to maintain altitude, what with your ship damaged. Correct?'

"'Yessir.' Again, the feeling of anxiety, of knowing that I'd done something really wrong.

"'Son, when you gave the order to drop your cargo, you were over neutral territory. You wiped out a civilian town. You destroyed a schoolhouse full of children, a church, a hospital, several of the local residents' homes; just about everything that lived inside that town is now dead. Do you understand?'

"I tried to speak, but the knot in my throat swelled up, and I couldn't respond. Civilians...I'd bombed a town of fucking civilians. Peasants that wanted nothing more than peace and protection from Hitler's fury, and I sent them to Hell with my bombs a'flying. And at that moment, something inside me snapped. I curled into a fetal position and cried like a baby. The general watched me for some time before he spoke again.

"'There are no charges pending against you, son...You did the best you could in a no-win situation. And based on your excellent record, we'll have you up and flying again in no time. But for now, you are grounded until the doctors say you're okay to fly again.'

"He turned and walked away, and the only sound burning in my ears was the sound of my blubbering and wailing. It was too much. I could see the images of children in my mind, being blown apart like rag dolls stuffed with firecrackers.

"But it didn't really hit home, really sink into my brain, until I read about it in the following morning's newspaper. The headline read, 'Scottish Lion Feeds On Neutral

Grounds!' I didn't get past the first paragraph of the story, the one that shouted out my name and the horrible mistake I'd made. My stomach clenched in knots, and I fought back being sick. My brain ached with the sound of falling bombs and the screams of dying children, I fell out of bed and onto my knees in prayer.

"Only, I didn't pray to God.

"I simply ranted.

"'I'll do anything, ANYTHING to get the hell out of here and go home. ANYTHING! I'll even sell my soul to the Devil to make this all end!'

"And it did. The very next morning I got my walking papers. Honorable Discharge, all my points earned. The Devil himself had answered my prayer. And iniquity followed me from that day forward."

5

My own sins. Even as I sit here recalling Mal's story, I find my mind drifting back into the past. I think I'm realizing now that time does not erase them. Time only casts shadows on them. Hides them. And as time goes by, as these sins are committed and concealed, those shadows fill the soul with darkness.

It's no wonder this world is filled with people that never find happiness. So many souls filled with the blackness of past sins festering inside them. They parade around day to day, searching for something to fill themselves with goodness and light. And at the end of the day, when their fruitless searching reaches its end, they fall deeper into despair.

It terrifies me to realize that I'm one of those people.

Looking back, I remember one sunny afternoon after my Sunday school class. I had been only nine or ten years old at the time. I was standing outside the church, waiting for my parents to meet me after mass had ended. Standing there, I noticed the garden of tulips growing around the sign post that read, "Our

Lady of Angels Church, est. 1908." I remember how pretty they were, and how happy I thought my mother would be if I picked some for her. I remember smiling as I walked up and down the rows of fiery reds, yellows, and purples; the way the honey bees buzzed carelessly about; the warm, fragrant scent of those beautiful flowers, blooming under the warm spring sun.

I remember how mad my mother was when she saw me standing there with those goddamn tulips in my hand.

"What you are doing, young man, is stealing," she yelled at me in front of all the other churchgoers as they left service and shuffled off to their cars. "...And stealing is a sin!"

I stood there, softly crying, my face burning with shame.

"I thought it would make you happy," I offered. My watering eyes looked down at those flowers, watching their beauty somehow manage to fade away.

"Let me tell you something, young man," she scolded as she grabbed my arm and dragged me toward our car. "The road to Hell is paved with good intentions. You just remember that next time you start to do something foolish."

Through the whole ordeal, my father never said a word. He only watched passively, a sad look spread out over his face. Looking back now, I remember our eyes meeting briefly, for the fraction of a second, before he got into the driver's seat. If the eyes really are the window to the soul, then I realize now that my father was a man filled with shadows.

Jump-cut to the fall of 1979. My sophomore year of college, and subsequently, the year I met Laura, the woman that would become the ex-Mrs. Blake. She was a junior at the time, and had already declared Business as her major. I was undeclared, but gearing toward English, with a Philosophy minor. Nobody really knows what they want to do with their life at that age. I figured a Liberal Arts degree was as good as anything else. Probably easier than Science or Math. At the time, I believed that any idiot who could read and write could manage to bullshit their way to a Liberal Arts degree. Of course, a Liberal Arts degree won't get you very far in Maine, unless you plan on becoming a teacher or have the higher aspirations of becoming a writer. I, of course, became neither.

Laura was the most beautiful girl I'd ever seen. She sat beside me in an art class we shared that September. It was an Introduction to Drawing course, which used nude models for subject matter. I remember the first model we had for the class; a rather plump, unattractive woman in her mid-thirties. While Laura was sketching the model, I began sketching *her.*

It was a fantastic likeness of her. I managed to capture the way her long, flowing hair spilled down her neck and shoulders; the way the light from the windows managed to shimmer in her eyes; the way her lips curled delicately into a smile as the charcoal pencil she used flew across her pad of paper.

I remember how her cheeks blushed when I showed her my picture. We ended up having dinner together that night. Our first date.

I remember how scared and angry I was when she told me she was pregnant that November. She wanted an abortion. Being a Catholic, I wouldn't stand for it.

Through the entire month, we argued and debated over what we thought we should do.

In the end, we eloped just before Christmas, neither of us telling our families. We both dropped out of college at the end of that semester. Myself to find a steady job to support my family. Her to start a home and raise our son when he was born.

Looking back now, I realize that if her life had been a flower, I had thoughtlessly plucked it away from her. In its place, seeds of regret were sown, and over the thirteen years we were married, weeds of resentment grew around everything that was once beautiful about her.

These are the shadows of my soul. And with them ring the sound of my mother's voice, reminding me that the road to Hell is paved with good intentions. All this I remembered as Mal's story continued...

6

"I bought this building with the money I'd saved during my time in the war. It was nothing like the money you'd expect to spend today if you were to buy a building like it. I bought it from a fellow that had originally used the lower portion, the part that is the bar you are sitting in, as a fish market. He'd lost his customers primarily to the Bentson Seafood Company, which had monopolized the fishing industry by exploiting the local fisherman, offering them health insurance on top of competitive wages. B.S.C. folded around a decade ago, and all the fisherman were left to struggle like the proverbial fish out of water.

"So this fellow folds, himself, and practically gives me the building to pay off his debts. And with a little spit and elbow grease, I built 'MacAuley's of Scotland.' Named after my own clan, I built not just a bar, but an establishment. Christ, what else does a god do after slaughtering innocent lambs? He builds a shrine and drinks the wine, baby. And more importantly, why does he drink? He drinks to forget.

"The most amazing thing about my bar...what separates it from any other bar in the world? The clientele that come in here today look exactly like the ones that came in fifty years ago. This bar is one giant time capsule, safe from the greasers of the fifties, the hippies of the sixties, the disco bunnies of the seventies, and the hipsters of the eighties. They never set foot in here. No sociological explanation, no geographic theories, no godly reason in our known universe is regulating them from walking through those doors. They just stay away, as if that stained glass window is some form of talisman of evil. I can see by that look on your face that I'm losing you...let me explain.

"The greasers, the hippies, the disco bunnies, and the hipsters all have their sinful devices, but that doesn't mean that they are evil in nature. But if you want ruthless, lawless, shameless, and downright evil...It's the businessmen every time. The ones who backstab to climb up the corporate ladders, the ones that exploit humanity for profit, the ones who willingly bend laws and corrupt the system, letting murderers and rapists run free in our city instead of making them face justice. They all bow to the almighty dollar sign, and they all find their way here, where they drink to their good health and fortune after spreading their corruption like a plague. And I smile and serve them drinks and take their dirty money like some kind of whore.

"So I'm no better. Hell, when I first opened for business, I had a guy come in here for drinks. He'd picked up some broad that obviously wasn't his wife, and I could tell he planned to schlep this girl, the way he was pawing all over her. So he offers me twenty dollars to use my apartment upstairs so they can do their business. Back then, twenty bucks was a lot of money, so I handed him the key, and he passed me a clean, fresh bill. And in that transaction, I felt like I'd been the father of original sin, opening the doors to a million shady deals that would transgress during my ownership of Mac's. And even then I could hear the sound of my voice, turning my soul over to Satan for what was behind door number three. So I'd drink more booze to drown out that voice.

"And a million shady deals did go down, right here in this very room you're sitting in. Hitmen have been hired in this room. Adultery has been committed here. And drug deals, con jobs, all kinds of dirty deeds. How about that for a legacy?

"But the worst for me was the seventies, when the Mafia started hanging around the joint. They acted as if they'd owned this place, with all sorts of gambling and whoring, and drugs and so forth. They had a prostitute named Mindy, a sweet young girl that put Ursula to shame... And I know how much you like Ursula, staring at her tits the way you do... Well, Mindy would turn tricks up in my apartment, and the Mafia boys offered me a cut of the profits and 'protection,'—as if I needed it with good ole' Satan backing me up. But when Mindy got pregnant by one of her Johns, they sent ME upstairs with the coat hanger to fix her. I can still smell the blood on my hands and in my kitchen sink where I tried to wash it off. I was, after all, the 'Scottish Lion.'

"By the time the eighties came around, I had boozed myself into being the biggest lush this side of New England. I'd practically be pouring free drinks on Thursdays and Fridays. And 'Hail, Hail, the gang's all here!' And in that boozy coma, I'd forgotten all about my promise to Satan. It didn't matter, and *if* I had to go to Hell, I'd go with a highball in one hand and a loose broad with big titties in the other. I rode that bull right up till 1990. And forty-five years after MacAuley's officially opened for business, I fell off the bull.

"Pushed off, actually, by a whole new thought pattern. I found myself asking *what if there is no Devil?* What if it was just a giant coincidence that I was sent home from the war after uttering that awful prayer? What if these forty-five years of sin that seemed to engulf my world like a hungry parasite is all on account of me believing I was already damned? What if God's grace is really amazing enough to redeem a sinner like me? I fell down on my knees before falling asleep that night, and I prayed to God for mercy and salvation.

"Just as I had when I prayed during the end of my time in the war, I got an answer the next day, in the form of a man."

7

"**H**e came into my bar and walked to this back corner, right where we're sitting. The guy was dressed entirely in black…but not like the other businessmen that come in here. He was wearing a long, flowing robe, and some sort of hat with a veil draped over to conceal his face. Christ, I thought someone I knew was playing a friggin' joke on me or something. But the really weird part was that no one else in the room seemed to notice him. He just floated right past them, and not a one of 'em looked up from their beers and took notice. I was dumbfounded. How the hell this guy dressed like it was Halloween could pass through a room full of men and not get laughed at is almost miraculous.

"So I walk over to him, not exactly sure what to say to the fellow, and hoping that I hadn't gone crazy or something. I get up to the table before Ursula can wait on him—if she even noticed him—and asked him, 'Can I help you, Pal?'

"'Sit down with me, Malcolm MacAuley.' That was how he answered.

"His voice was so damn strange, as if he'd gargled with sulfuric acid and broken glass. It came out in a mix between a growl and a hiss, but it managed to sound pleasant all the same. The guy was freaking me out. He knew my name.

"'I own this place, and I'll be the one to give orders. Now, how 'bout taking that

stupid mask off so I can see your face?'

"'I don't think you understand,' he hissed out. He lifted an old, wrinkled hand into the air, and the room fell dead. Not dead as in deceased, but everything and everybody froze in mid-action. It was as if my bar was some sort of wax museum, and my clients were nothing more than mannequins, posed in some bizarre diorama that only I could see. I glanced around and saw each individual the way he was frozen. Old Kenny Tyler was guzzling down a beer, his free hand holding a cigar—even the smoke rising from it was frozen still. Paul Jennings was leaning over the pool table, his cue stick just setting the ball in motion, but the ball was standing still inches away from the tip. Judge Philips was in mid story at a table with three lawyers, although I don't recall their names, but they were frozen with laughs and smiles plastered on their faces. In the back of the bar, Steven was pouring a pitcher of beer, but the beer flowing from the tap was standing dead still. Ursula was leaning over another table of customers, taking phantom orders as each of the men seemed to be frozen at eye level with her breasts. I swear to

God, it looked like a goddamn Norman Rockwell painting. I looked back at the figure at the table, and sat down across from him.

"'That's better,' he said.

"'Who are you?' I asked in a voice that must have sounded confused and frightened as hell.

"'Forgive me for not introducing myself. There are those in the bible who have named me Adam. I have not gone by that name in ages, though. I was him, when I was of the flesh as you are. I am the Angel of Death.'

"The figure nodded at me from behind the black veil, and I felt a chilling touch of horror pouring through my body.

"'And you, Malcolm MacAuley,' his wrinkled old finger drew into a point directed at me, '…you are in peril beyond your capacity to understand.'

"'If you're an angel, how come you ain't wearing white? And how come there ain't no trumpets playing and a choir of angels behind you singing praise to God? Isn't that the way it's supposed to be? And what's with the veil? I ain't allowed to see your face or something?' The questions came, but I don't recall them ever even passing my mind. They just fell out of my mouth before I knew what I was saying.

"'Those who see my face are the ones that die, and I lead their souls to the throne of judgment. If I show you my face now, sir, you will stand before His throne, and you'll be cast into Hell. There are angels singing as we speak, and trumpets sounding from the heavens…But your soul is tainted as black as night, and so you cannot hear them.'

"My body went as weak as jelly, and I slumped back against the seat. I was afraid.

More scared in my life than words could ever express. But worse than that, I felt dirty.

Not my skin on the outside, but my soul on the inside. I could feel it. I could feel blackness oozing out of every pore on my body. The only thing I could do was to ask it questions, in the hope of buying myself time.

"'If you are the Angel of Death, how did you become that? How did you get such a fantastic job?'

"The figure nodded again.

"'Be patient, and I will explain all. As I've told you, in the flesh, I was Adam. I fathered original sin on this earth. And my wife, Eve, partnered. From our own weakness came every sin and darkness this world has known. You see, God created the universe, and everything within. And he created us. And we were the ones who created sin. All violence, wars, hunger, disease, suffering, they are our doing. When people grow sick with terminal diseases, or when terrible accidents happen, or when famine destroys an entire nation, people ask how a loving God could create these catastrophes. God doesn't. He only watches to see how these people react to such tragedy, how strong their faith is, and decides their judgment accordingly when they die. But he is not the inventor of sin. God is most holy and perfect, and will not create such unholy imperfections.

"'Our penance for our sins in the Garden of Eden was based on service to God

My own service is to be the Angel of Death. I am and have been present at the death of every mortal on this planet since creation. I let them look upon my face at their death, and lead them to the throne of judgment. I have witnessed every agony this world has known and suffered. In a way, that is my punishment. I was present when The Son Jesus was crucified. I lead him to the throne myself, blinded in his radiant glory. Eve's punishment is that she was to mother every form of malady and suffering this world has known. She is the author of all diseases, famines, wars, and natural disasters. In a way, her punishment is worse than my own, but then, she was the one to be deceived by Satan.

"'I was there when your bombs fell, and I collected the souls of the lives you destroyed. I saw the horror in their faces, the tears in their eyes. They looked upon my face, and I led them to the throne of judgment in His holy court. Some had known Jesus, the Christ, and were righteous at heart. Those were the ones admitted into the kingdom of Heaven. Others had not known him, had turned away from His holy words, and were cast into the deepest pits of Hell. There were many children among them, of those lives you destroyed.'

"'I didn't mean to kill them,' I said. 'It was an accident...I would have died had I not pushed the bombs out of my plane. They were weighing us down...'

"'That is not why your soul is damned, Malcolm MacAuley!' His voice had stiffened, and it rang in my ears. I was trembling, now.

"'The Lord tested Job's faith with several tragedies, but Job's faith could not be moved. You were tested in a similar manner. At first, you were humble, and your faith was strong. Before you were called to war, you were of very strong faith. You heard and accepted God's word on the Sabbath. Before you left the war, your faith was shattered, and you prayed to Satan, offering your soul to be relieved from your duties. That...' his gnarled finger pointed at me again, emphasizing his words. 'That is why your soul is damned.'

"My eyes filled with tears. I was overwhelmed with fear and sadness, all mixed into a blackness darker than any moonless night. It choked me, filling my every breath with malodorous pitch until my lungs ached and burned. And before I could contemplate all the things swimming around in my brain, my voice wailed in sheer agony.

"'God have mercy on me!'

"The figure across from me held up his hand, signaling me to silence myself.

I looked at him and could see his eyes burning from somewhere behind the veil that covered his face. I brushed the tears from my cheeks, my eyes meeting his.

"'So, what are you here for, then?'

"'Last night you prayed for mercy and forgiveness. The Lord God has chosen to answer your prayer. He forgives you of your sins. However, in your case, it is not enough.'

"'Not enough?'"

8

"**Y**ou still with me, kid?"

Mal was looking up at me, his hand curled around his glass of beer like a tight, iron fist. His face was equally tense, as I'm sure the rest of him probably was despite the quantity of beer he'd been drinking.

"Yeah," I sighed. "Only I get the feeling you're making half this shit up just to get me to calm down."

Mal tipped his head back and guzzled down the rest of his beer. He threw a careless arm across his mouth and sleeved off the spillage, and stood up.

"I think I need a refill before we go on. How about yourself?"

I shook my head. My glass was only half empty (or half full, if you're an optimist).

I took a small sip and watched him shuffle behind the counter and refill his glass under the bar tap. He blew the foamy head off and tapped out a few more drops. One of the other patrons noticed him behind the bar and ran up to order another drink, which Mal was glad to refill. When he finished, he rang up the fellow's drink and came back to the table.

"Ya see that guy I just waited on?"

"Yeah, what about him?"

"He's been coming to this bar for over thirty years. Thirty years! Shit, he first started coming here right before the 'Summer of Love,' when everyone else his age was wearing tie-dyes and bell bottoms, and driving off to Woodstock instead of going off to Vietnam. No, this kid was a law student. I'll never forget it. He came in here for the first time to celebrate passing his bar exam. He was with some girl or other when he came in, and since then he's had some girl or other with him through his whole career as a lawyer. But look at him now. He's in his fifties, he's got no wife or kids…he'll retire soon and die a lonely man. And he's made a fortune defending thugs and perverts and every type of lawlessness under the sun. And more than half of them were guilty as sin, and deserved to go to prison, but he found loopholes and technicalities. Yup, very successful and very rich. But you know what? He can't take it with him when he goes."

I glanced over at the fellow. He looked tired and wrinkled, and very lonely. Perhaps he was rich, but his days of partying and cavorting with little girls was long gone. He had the look that every homeless person has out on the streets. The kind you see every day, sitting out on the sidewalks and sleeping under bridges. The look that says, "I could be you someday. Have mercy on me. After all, I am a human being." It's written in their sad eyes, and chiseled into their tired mouths, which seem to have forgotten how to smile. For a brief second, I felt as if I might be looking at an older version of myself.

"Shall I continue with my story?" Mal was seated again, his eyes watching me watch the other fellow at the end of the bar. I nodded, and took another sip of beer.

9

"Not enough?' I asked.

"'Not enough,' he repeated. 'You have married iniquity, and it has betrayed you as only the Devil himself knows how. He has a place reserved for you in Hell, and he's quite anxious to take your soul. He's watching us right now...'

"My eyes swept across the bar, but I could only see the frozen faces of my customers. The Usual Gang of Idiots, as old Alfred E. Neuman would have called 'em. All of them sat silent now; hardly a possibility if you'd asked me before my mysterious guest had arrived.

"'Not that you can see him,' my mysterious guest added, watching my eyes glance about the room. 'But he's waiting for you to keep your promise. God forgives you for your sins, but he can't accept you into Heaven if it means breaking your promise. For righteousness can never be tainted. If I took you before the throne of judgment, you'd still be damned.'

"'Is Hell bad? Is it a lake of fire, like they say in the Bible?'

"'It is that and more. It is pain and fear and sadness and everything black. And it grows. With every soul that enters, it grows in size and strength. It will continue to grow until the gates of Hell have reached this world. And the angels in Heaven will sound trumpets, and Armageddon will begin. It is written in the Book of Revelation, and will begin first with the Rapture, where all the righteous will ascend into Heaven without dying. They will be God's army against evil. Then the Horsemen shall ride into this world. It has all been prophesied.'

"'Will God's army win?'

"'Righteousness and perfection will never be thwarted. And blessed are the people called to fight for it. They will sing praise to God's glory in the kingdom of Heaven. But woe to the soldiers of evil. There will be great wailing and gnashing of teeth. And woe to this world, for it will be destroyed so that the gates of Hell may be closed forever.'

"I listened in horror as these things were told to me. The end of the world and the final battle between good and evil. I was terrified, with the echoes of his words in my ears and the pounding of my own heart within my chest. I almost preferred not to know.

"'When will all this happen?'

"'Perhaps within your lifetime, perhaps the next generation. It is only for Him to know. But it will be soon. Satan's army multiplies every day. As I've told you, he has a place waiting for you among his legions.'

"Tears filled my eyes.

"'I want to be righteous! I want to serve God! Please, please have mercy on my soul. I'm truly sorry for my sins.' I begged like a child, my words falling out of my mouth faster than my brain could think them up. In my life, I had known sadness and fear, but this was my mortality on a thread, and I cried for God to throw me a rope.

"'I do not doubt your sincerity, Malcolm MacAuley. That is why I have come for you. I am going to make you an offer.'

"An offer I can't refuse is what ran through my mind, complete with a nasally

Marlon Brando voice. I held my silence and listened.

"'As I've said. Service to God has been my punishment and penance for my sins.

My service is near completion, that I may enter the kingdom of Heaven and sing praise to God in his glory. When this happens, I must be replaced.'

"I knew immediately what he was going to say. I could have seen it coming had I not been so busy fearing for my life.

"'Your soul may be redeemed by such service. And there is no other way. God will purify your soul, and your promise to Satan will melt away like wax. You shall take my place as the Angel of Death.'

"'You want me to be the Angel of Death?' It sounded so ludicrous that I had to hold back a laugh, despite how terrified I was. 'You want me to watch people die? I don't think I can do that.' In all my years of owning this bar, and all my years of hiding away from the atrocities I caused during the war, I couldn't remember a more sinister or morbid request. And I'd already heard and seen it all.

"'It is the only way,' the figure before me reiterated. His voice seemed to crawl beneath my skin, clawing and pinching my nerves. His eyes still burned beneath the veil, and I was beginning to wonder if this wasn't really Satan himself in disguise.

"'I can't give you an answer today…I need time to think this over,' which was true. You don't just jump into the role of the Angel of Death. It made me wonder if there was some sort of training course for it in some angel school somewhere in some other world. 'You can give me time, can't you? I wasn't scheduled to die today was I?' The thought slapped me back to reality. He hadn't mentioned it yet, but if he wanted to, he could very easily have taken my soul with him that evening. And with the wonderful prospect of the Devil already owning my soul, it didn't hurt to try and buy more time.

"In the grand scheme of things, you'd think I'd have jumped at the chance to save my soul from damnation. I certainly don't want to burn for all eternity. But the enormous consequences involved, the implications are staggering. How would you like to be the person in charge of watching every other person on the face of this earth die? How would you like to be the one to lead them to the throne of judgment? How would you like to watch people being sent to Hell? But mostly, what if you knew those people and loved them? What if they were your own children, Frank? Would you like to see your own children die? Can you possibly imagine how many people die every day? Hundreds, thousands, tens and hundreds of thousands. And in at least a million different ways. And it would be your job to collect these peoples souls, as if they were nothing more than objects you'd throw in your pocket. Could you live with those terms?

"The figure sat silently across from me. I could feel the weight of his proposal crushing me, until my soul was too heavy for my body to carry. I started crying. Blubbering like a little fucking kid, with runners of snot hanging out of my nose. I was lost for words. How do you tell an angel how dirty you feel? Or how entirely alone? I think I was waiting for him to tell me not to be afraid, like angels are supposed to when they make important announcements. He didn't, though. He just sat there watching me. Finally he spoke.

"'Very well, Malcolm MacAuley. The offer has been presented. My own service is almost through. I will return again when it is complete. Your flesh will come to its end on that day, and a decision will be required of you. I recommend you weigh your choices carefully. The glory of God is unparalleled, and the pains of Hell are as well. God is calling you to service. If you should deny, your fate is forever sealed in burning agony. People die every day, whether you are present or not. You cannot change that fact. Nor can you change their judgment before the throne of God. But you can show them mercy, and help them not to be afraid.'

"The phantom before me rose to his feet and turned toward the door.

"'Weigh your decision carefully, Malcolm MacAuley...Your soul depends on it.'

"He walked toward the door, but, like some unwanted ghost, his body faded into shadows and disappeared before it could reach the door handle. The moment he was completely gone, the room snapped back to life as if nothing happened. And none of the people in the room seemed to see me at this back table, crying and praying for mercy."

10

"**S**o what are you going to do?" I asked. "Have you made a decision?"

Mal shook his head.

"Kid, I've thought more about this than you can possibly imagine. The only thing that I'm really sure about is that I'm terrified of dying. I've been to the doctor for periodic checkups. I stopped drinking and smoking so heavily, not that I quit entirely either. I even bought a copy of the Bible and started reading it. I'm somewhere in the New Testament right now, and I'm hoping to finish Revelation before I die. I even started going to church again. But as much as I do to right my wrongs, I can still hear his voice telling me, 'It's the only way.' I really fucked things up for myself. I guess what it boils down to is that I'll only know my final decision after I've made it. When he comes for me again, I'll just blurt out my answer."

I nodded. It sounded like the sanest approach I could think of. At least that way he could dwell on his situation as little as possible until his life was finished.

"But I'll tell you this," he continued. "I've been watching the obituaries like a hawk. And every day I see at least one name I recognize. If not someone I knew in my life, then some celebrity, or politician, or athlete, or criminal put to death. Every day is some car accident, or plane crash, or burning building, or gang violence, and people die. And each and every one of them has some sin or other buried deep down in their hearts. Out of all these people, I'm the one who was offered a clean slate. You're going to die someday, Frank...I'll have been dead long before you, but I'll still be around to take your soul away from you. How 'bout another beer while you ponder that one?"

He pointed at my empty glass. I'd finished it during his story but was far too intrigued to ask for a refill. I watched him carry his glass and my own back to the bar to pour us each a fresh cold one. The man at the end of the bar noticed him up again, and ran over for a refill as well. Mal took his glass and filled it, but instead of collecting money, Mal waved his hand and told him, "On the house." He was smiling when he came back to our table.

"Same for you," he said, "On the house."

I thanked him.

"You know, I feel better after finally getting that off my chest. It's been quite a burden to carry that around for so long. I've spent fifty years listening to other peoples' problems. I'm glad someone could finally listen to mine."

I offered a smile and a shrug. I wasn't sure if he was telling the truth or if his story was so much hot air to get me to cool off. He must have read it on my face.

"You think I'm full of shit, don't you? Well, I suppose you have a right to. Who in this world would ever believe a story like that from a crazy old man who's heard more bullshit in his life than he deserves? Well, who knows? Maybe it will make a dent in you after all, and you'll forgive your ex-wife for the shit she's done to you. Maybe it won't. But I'll tell you something... You'll think twice about things when you hear about my death. Maybe then it will all sink in, and if it's not too late, you'll forgive her."

"Maybe," I agreed, and drank my beer.

11

I had almost fallen into insanity when I bought the gun. I'd had a terrible nightmare during the nap I take between working at Harding and driving my cab. It had left me in a cold sweat, my heart pounding in my chest, my hands clenched into fists which shook at my sides. I somehow managed to get dressed in the dark and walked over to the pawn shop on Congress Street. I walked like a zombie, my eyes in a dead stare as the events in the nightmare continued to swim through my brain. It was the Monday after I heard Mal's story.

I dreamed I'd been driving my cab around the city. It was abysmally dark outside, like when you turn out the light in your bedroom, and for an agonizing instant, while your eyes are adjusting to the absence of light, everything is pitch black. Even the headlights of my cab could barely slice through and penetrate such darkness. As I drove, I saw Malcolm standing alone on a street corner. He saw me, and a sad smile lit across his chin. I pulled over and picked him up.

He'd been carrying a suitcase, which he shoved into the back seat before climbing in.

"You're running late, kid," he announced as he settled into the chapped leather of the back seat. "Take me to my bar."

I flicked the meter and pulled away from the curb.

This had been at the far side of the city. As I drove, I began to realize that we were in the only car on the street. In fact, there was not another person to be seen. On any given night, I would normally have passed dozens of cars and countless pedestrians moving about after the local bars had closed for the night. Even the homeless people, normally slumbering through a haze of cheap liquor out on the sidewalks were gone.

Just the two of us.

And the inky, demon-like shadows that began to float by the windows of my cab. I glanced at my fare in the rearview mirror.

"What's going on here, Mal?"

He had opened his suitcase and started rummaging through it.

"Pay no attention to 'em." He responded. "Just drive on."

I continued to drive, but my eyes were looking into that terrible darkness, watching these phantasms float by. Other than a pair of burning red eyes, they had no facial features. Nor were they carried by legs. They appeared to hover and glide along through midair as they circled my cab.

They were following us. And as we progressed in our journey, more and more would join in this ghostly parade.

I glanced again at Mal through the rearview mirror. He had pulled a long, black robe out of his suitcase and slipped it on. I noticed that somehow, the skin of his hands and face had aged a great deal in a matter of minutes. Spider webs of wrinkles had spread across his flesh; his neck and cheeks were bloated out in thick, pudgy folds. His eyes were sinking into their sockets, so that only tiny bits of his pupils were showing.

Mal was dying right before my eyes.

I was on the verge of altering my route, to take Mal to a hospital, when he spoke again.

"The bar, Francis...bring us to the bar." It was like he was reading my mind.

"But you're sick..." My eyes shifted uneasily from the mirror to the road. The phantasms had continued to double and triple. I could now hear their shrieks and moans through the thin glass windows of my cab.

"I'm already dead," Mal announced from the back seat. "...And so are you."

A chill of terror seized me. I could not speak, could barely breathe, as this revelation was passed to me.

I glanced again in the mirror. Mal donned a long, black veil that now concealed his face completely. I watched while the figure in black that had once been my friend closed the suitcase and sat in silence as our journey continued.

"You already know too much," the figure finally announced out loud, his voice no longer sounding like Mal's, but rather a deep, throaty growl that made my skin crawl.

"So I shall tell you the rest. These shadows that follow us...they are the souls of the damned. They are the souls that are cast out of Heaven on their judgment day. They are stained black with evil and sin, and are devoid of any humanity they once possessed.

"Why are they following us?" I asked in a whisper, as if afraid they might hear me. My eyes followed them as they floated and danced around my cab.

"They aren't following us, really..." The figure answered. "They are on their way to the bar. Don't you know by now, the bar is a magnet for evil?"

I shook my head. My heart was racing inside my chest, my sweaty palms clinging to the steering wheel.

"It has drawn you there. You didn't find the bar. The bar found *you*. It felt the evil inside you and pulled you to it. Pretty soon, you will have to join these shadows outside."

Tears began to well up in my eyes, and I could feel their cold, salty sting as they rolled down my cheeks and across my lips.

"Let me redeem myself," I whispered. "Surely there's still time..."

"It is too late for you," the Angel of Death (my mind could name it now) replied. "You have murdered your wife. And you have damned her soul as well. She waits for you at the bar. But not to join you. She means to eat your soul when she finds you. She has become cannibal, and waits for your corpse."

The shadows were now attacking my cab. From all around us came the sounds of long, razor-sharp fingernails scraping away at the metal and glass. The sounds of screaming and wailing pierced the darkness in some awful, malignant chorus.

I stopped the cab and turned to my friend.

"I didn't murder her! I only wanted to."

"That was enough," he said.

"And it isn't my fault she was damned. She made her own choices. I refuse to accept responsibility!"

The figure in the backseat chuckled.

"Your wedding vows..." He was pointing a long, crooked finger at me. "They meant nothing to you. Love, honor, cherish. All these things you took for granted. All you did was take until she had nothing left to give. In your own selfishness, you drained all the love out of her heart. You left her empty. Her only recourse was to find another to show her love. You drove her away, and that forced her into adultery."

My chin fell open, but no words came out. I stepped on the gas and drove on.

"Ah, we're almost there," the figure said aloud. "But let me finish this revelation. Your children are also damned. Without your loving guidance and discipline, your son will become just like you. He will use up women and leave them empty, just as you have with his mother. He will die alone, just as you have. And he will never know love; only hatred and rage. And your daughter will be just like her mother. She will never be able to differentiate between love and sex. She will sleep with men who will only show physical affections, and ultimately she will succumb as a result. She, too, will never know love, and will die with an empty heart and an unclean soul."

We pulled up in front of MacAuley's of Scotland. My eyes were burning so badly from the tears that I could hardly see.

"I see your wife is here waiting for you." The Angel of Death lifted his hand and pointed a finger at the crowd of souls gathered around the door of the bar.

"It would be best if you beat her into the bar," he continued. "If you make it through the door before she catches you, there's a good chance you'll never see her again."

I turned and looked at the back of my cab. The figure in the black veil began to disappear.

"Goodbye, Francis Blake," it said as it winked out of existence.

"Goodbye, Malcolm MacAuley," I said. Then I was out the door.

I charged blindly through the crowd of spirits. My teeth clenched, my arms out in front of me, I ran as fast as my legs could carry me. I could see the spirit of my ex-wife rise above the others and race toward me. I could tell it was her, although the beauty that her features once held were now gone. Only hateful, burning red eyes and savage, razor-sharp teeth that she meant to tear my soul apart with. As my feet raced forward, I watched in terror while she somehow managed to close the gap between myself and the door. I could feel hope fade away, and a wave of fear and dread washed through my veins.

I closed my eyes and barreled through the door of the bar.

I was not inside MacAuley's of Scotland. The door had closed behind me before I even noticed that I was ankle-deep in a lake of fire.

Hellfire.

The bar had become the center of Hell. It was drawing me in, consuming me, feeding off the evil I had done and using it to burn me. Miles and miles of burning flames and molten lava surrounded me, engulfing my flesh. My last screams and cries echoed in my ears, but they were nowhere near loud enough to drown out the pain.

And then I was awake.

Darkness had already set in as I staggered down the street toward the pawn shop. It was a frightening experience. All that time I had spent planning to kill my ex-wife, when everything that happened had been my own damn fault.

I purchased a .38 revolver and a box of bullets. I dropped a wad of loose cash, my watch, and my gold wedding band (which I had not worn since the divorce but kept in my wallet) on the counter. There were no questions asked as I took my purchase and slowly plodded out the door and wandered back to my apartment.

By that point, only one thought passed through my mind.

This was all my fault. I have to end this. This is the only way!

I remember sitting on my couch and loading the gun. I remember how the smooth wooden handle of the gun felt in my hand and the cold steel barrel as I loaded each chamber, knowing that all I really needed was one bullet. And with tears in my eyes, I placed the barrel in my mouth and cocked the hammer, waiting to see if I was man enough to pull the trigger.

12

Today is my daughter's eighteenth birthday. Child support officially ends today, although I've saved up some money over the last few years to help her with college. The restraining order has also been dropped, so I am taking her out to lunch to celebrate. I'm so proud of her. She is graduating at the top of her class, and has been accepted into Harvard. And she's so beautiful. She looks a lot like her mother did when we first started dating. Her older brother is already in college, although his marks weren't that terrific, and he ended up in a local community college. He isn't lazy… he tries very hard in his studies, but has difficulty grasping a lot of the material presented in his courses.

My ex-wife and I are on speaking terms again. As I'd suspected, her lawyer boyfriend's departure really burned her good. My son told me she had a nervous breakdown after she'd found out about his affair (I didn't tell her), and ended up kicking him out of the house. I've seen Joshua once or twice driving around the city in his new Porsche, which I'm sure he could afford with all the money he saved by freeloading off my wife. I actually pulled my cab up beside him at a stop light one time. He was on my right, and I could see the young blonde that was with him when he entered Mac's that night four long years ago. He turned and saw me smiling at him, and his face turned bright red, his chin falling in dismay. I was deciding if I wanted to give him a fender bender, my cab against his expensive sports car, but before I could, he threw on his directional signal and made a right on red. And wouldn't you know it, it was a 'no turn on red' zone, and the vehicle behind him was a police car. I watched in my rearview as the officer walked over to his car, pulling out his ticket book from his back pocket. Poor Josh looked miserable. I'm sure he had a friend somewhere to help him squash the ticket, but I was satisfied enough at the inconvenience he went through just to avoid me.

As I've said, my ex and I are talking again. I told her I forgave her for all she had done to me, and that I wished her well. It must have sounded sincere, too, because she started crying and apologizing left and right for all the shit she'd done to me. She went so far as to ask if we could maybe start over and be a family again. I told her I needed time to consider it. It will be a long time before I can trust her again, that I'm sure. We started going to church together on Sundays. I'd forgotten how much I used to enjoy spending time with her, and I think she feels the same way.

I miss my friend Malcolm very much, and I believe that he's played a great part in my "healing." I'm finding an inner peace that has overcome the turmoil in my life. My faith in God has grown, and I feel that my spiritual relationship with Him has led me to salvation. I am a better person for it. Mal had mentioned a question he'd asked himself in his story; about whether God's grace was amazing enough to save a sinner like me. I believe it is. I also believe that when I die, the Angel of Death will offer me a beer before my journey to the throne of judgment.

MacAuley's of Scotland was left to both Steven and Ursula, as accorded in Mal's

Will. Things went on pretty much the same after Mal's death. Same clients, same shady deals and dark secrets. But within a month after his death, Mac's caught on fire and burned to the ground. Some speculate that one of the two heirs of the establishment set the place on fire to collect the insurance money, although arson could not be proven. Nobody was injured in the blaze, but I suspect Mal might have been there all the same. I can't help but wonder if he might have started the blaze himself, just to destroy the shrine he'd built out of sin. The building itself burned like hellfire. I'd caught a glimpse of it from my cab as I arrived to drive people home during my shift. I watched as the stained-glass window exploded under the intense heat, spraying shards of colored glass into the night air. I watched as the fire trucks rolled onto the scene just a minute too late to do anything but spray the surrounding buildings, to keep them from burning as well.

Only Mac's burned. And I watched it, wondering if that was what the gates of Hell looked like.

Peter N. Dudar is the Bram Stoker Award® nominated author of A REQUIEM FOR DEAD FLIES. His recent fiction can be found in the new anthology *Nightscapes, Volume 1* (also published by Nightscape Press) as well as the anthology *Bleed* (a charitable collection to raise money and awareness for the National Children's Cancer Society, sponsored by Perpetual Motion Machine Publishing). Dudar has also recently released his first collection, DOLLY, AND OTHER STORIES, published by Evil Jester Press. He currently writes a film review column for Cinema Knife Fight as well as maintaining a blog called *Dead By Friday* at Wordpress.com. Dudar lives in Lisbon Falls, Maine with his wife Amy and their two daughters, Vivian and Liliana. He is a proud member of the New England Horror Writers.

Made in the USA
Charleston, SC
16 June 2015